Stink

Megan McDonald   illustrated by

K and the Great Guinea Pig Express

Peter H. Reynolds

SCHOLASTIC INC.
New York Toronto London Auckland Sydney
Mexico City New Delhi Hong Kong Buenos Aires

The publisher wishes to express its gratitude to Kathy Anderson and Lyn Zantow for their insightful feedback regarding guinea pig adoption and the proper care of guinea pigs.

ISBN-13: 978-0-545-15626-4
ISBN-10: 0-545-15626-2

12 11 10 9 8 7 6 5 4 3 2 1   9 10 11 12 13 14/0

Printed in the U.S.A.   40

First Scholastic printing, April 2009

The book was typeset in Stone Informal and hand-lettered.
The illustrations were created digitally.

for Jordan
M. M.

To the entire staff of
The Blue Bunny bookshop
in historic Dedham Square
P. H. R.

CONTENTS

The Great Wall

Shake!

Rattle!

Squeal!

Stink could hardly see as he carried a Leaning Tower of Cereal Boxes up to Webster's front door. "Ding-dong," he called out.

"Whoa!" said Webster. "C'mon in. Sophie's here, too. This is going to be the most fun ever."

"How many cereal boxes did you collect?" Sophie asked.

"Umpteen," said Stink.

"All I brought was Cheerful O's," said Sophie of the Elves. "My dad says they're heart healthy."

"Carrying all these boxes is *not* heart healthy," said the out-of-breath Stink. "Why couldn't we just use sugar cubes?"

"Stink, we're building the Great Wall of China! Do you know how long it would take to build a wall out of teeny-tiny cubes?"

"Well, it took hundreds of years in real life," said Stink.

"Ours is only going to take one day," said Webster.

Just then, Stink's giant stack of cereal boxes crashed to the ground. "Somebody sure likes Mood Flakes!" said Webster.

"My sister, Judy," said Stink. "They change color when you pour milk on them."

"Weird!" said Webster.

"Interesting," said Sophie.

Stink pulled two shiny silver-gray rolls of tape out of his back pockets. "I brought super-sticky duck tape!"

"In our family, we call it goose tape," said Sophie. Stink and Webster cracked up. The three friends lined up the cereal boxes in the backyard and goose-taped them together.

"The Great Wall of Goose Tape!" said Stink. "Did you guys know that you can see the Great Wall from outer space?" He wondered if any aliens or Martians would be able to see the Great Wall of Cereal Boxes when it was done.

"The *real* Great Wall is more than

two thousand miles long," said Webster.

"We have about a thousand miles to go," said Sophie.

Webster stood up. His arm was stuck to Sophie. Sophie's shoe was stuck to Stink. Stink's shirt was stuck to Webster's sleeve.

"Oh, no!" said Sophie. "We're stuck to each other."

"Don't worry," said Stink. "Friends *should* stick together."

When they finally got unstuck, Stink looked at the Great Wall. He could not believe his eyes. The Great Wall was moving. The Great Wall was shaking. The Great Wall was quaking. "Look!" he said, pointing.

"Why is it *moving*?" asked Webster.

"Maybe it's the wind," said Sophie.

"Does the wind go *wee, wee, wee, wee, wee*?" asked Stink.

All three of them heard the squeaking sound now. *Wee, wee, wee, wee, wee.* "There it is again!" said Stink. "Something's inside the Great Wall!"

"Sounds like a baby bird," said Sophie.

"Or a creepy rat," said Webster.

Stink and his friends crawled on hands and knees through the grass. Stink peered into an empty box of Mood Flakes at one end. A furry hair ball with dark brown eyes, a wet pink nose, and twitchy whiskers peered back at him.

"All I found is . . . a guinea pig!" said Stink.

"I found one, too!" said Sophie.

"I found one, three!" said Webster.

STINK'S FURRY FACTS

THIS LITTLE RODENT WENT TO MARKET

A FUNNY BONE IS NOT A BONE.

HA HA HA!

A PRAIRIE DOG IS NOT A DOG.

A GUINEA PIG IS NOT A PIG — IT'S A RODENT.

OINK

NOT A GUINEA PIG →

UNLIKE RATS AND MICE, GUINEA PIGS ARE BORN WITH A FULL COAT OF HAIR, EYES WIDE OPEN, AND REALLY **BIG** FEET.

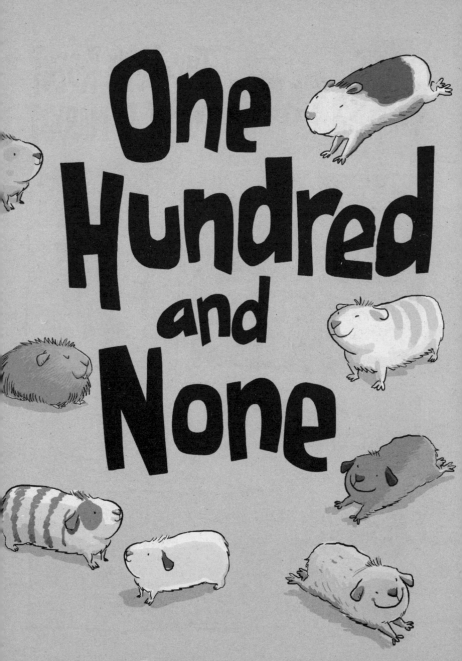

One Hundred and None

uinea pig party!" said Sophie, holding up a tricolor guinea pig that looked like it was wearing a wig.

"Guinea pig *palooza,*" said Webster, putting a black-and-white guinea pig in his lap.

"The Great Wall of Guinea Pigs!" said Stink, holding a little fur ball with blue eyes and spiky hair.

"When did you get three guinea pigs?" Sophie asked Webster.

"And how come you didn't tell us?" asked Stink.

"They're not mine," said Webster. "I never saw them before. I don't know *how* they got here."

"If we were at my house," said Stink, "I'd say my sister, Judy, was trying to clone guinea pigs again. One time, she put guinea pig hairs in the microwave to make more guinea pigs."

"Maybe they escaped from the circus," said Webster.

"Maybe they escaped from a mad scientist," said Sophie.

14

"Maybe they're alien guinea pigs from the planet Squeak," said Stink.

"They look like plain old earthlings to me," said Webster. He ran into his house to get an apple and some broccoli. The hungry guinea pigs munched down the apple in a flash.

"Eat all the broccoli, too," urged Webster. "So I won't have to."

"I'm calling mine Astro," said Stink.

"I'm calling mine Oreo," said Webster.

"We can't keep them," said Sophie. "They must belong to somebody."

"Yeah—us!" Webster said. "Finders keepers, losers weepers."

"Finders *stealers,* losers weepers," said Sophie.

"Let's take them to Fur & Fangs," said Stink. "Mrs. Birdwistle will know what we should do."

Webster and Sophie put their guinea pigs into a shoe box poked with holes. Stink let Astro ride in his very own shoe box.

When they got to Fur & Fangs, Stink could not believe his eyes. Or his ears. Cages were toppled every which way. Puppies squealed and parrots squawked. Rabbits raced in circles. And guinea pigs squeaked from every direction, running loose all over the shop.

"Don't just stand there," said Mrs. Birdwistle. "Help me catch them."

"Let the Great Guinea Pig Chase begin!" said Stink. Stink, Sophie, and Webster crawled on all fours, cooing in baby talk and coaxing guinea pigs back into their cages with parsley.

"We'll find the little hair balls if it takes till next Christmas!" said Webster.

When all the cages were right side up and all the piggies were safe inside again, Stink told Mrs. Birdwistle about finding three guinea pigs at Webster's house. "They must be escapees," he said.

"I'm not surprised," said Mrs. Birdwistle. "The latches on the cage doors were broken, and they've been running mad all morning. Better help me do a quick count."

". . . ninety-nine, one hundred, one hundred and one!" called Stink.

"They're all here!" said Mrs. B. "Including the three that went to see the Great Wall of China."

"Are you stocking up for a big blow-out guinea pig sale?" asked Sophie.

"Heavens, no," said Mrs. Birdwistle.

"I heard about these little critters on the news yesterday. A lab was using the poor things to test shampoo and perfume. They've been half starved to death, twenty or more jammed to a cage, and they were living in their own droppings." She pinched her nose. "Not pretty!"

"Yuck," said Webster. "That's really terrible."

"I couldn't stand to think of the poor little guys taken to a shelter," said Mrs. B. "If they're not adopted right away, they get put to sleep. So I marched down there and told Animal Control I'd take all one hundred and one guinea pigs. What in the world was I thinking?"

"Wow, you're like a guinea pig *superhero*," said Webster.

"Fantastic Fur Friend to the rescue!" said Stink.

"I wish I could make some of these guinea pigs disappear. Saving them is one thing. Finding one hundred and one good homes is another." Mrs. B. pulled some straw from her hair.

"We'll help," said Stink.

"We can ring doorbells around the neighborhood," said Webster.

"Ding-dong, guinea pigs calling," said Sophie of the Elves.

"That sounds great," Mrs. B. said. "For now, I'll have to keep them in the old camper out back. There's no room in here, and Mona Lisa the mynah bird is driving them crazy with her guinea pig imitations."

"*Wee, wee, wee, wee, wee!*" squawked Mona Lisa.

"*Wee, wee, wee, wee, wee!*" the guinea pigs squeaked back.

✳ ✳ ✳

The minute Stink got home, he told Judy about the 101 guinea pigs. "How many do you think Mom and Dad will let me keep?"

"Zero," said Judy. "As in one hundred and *none*."

"Not even one?" Stink asked. "There's this one guy with blue eyes and spiky black hair and—"

"Hel-lo!" Judy said. "Did you forget about Mouse? Do you really think a guinea pig is going to like living with a cat?"

Stink did not want to listen. He went to find Mom anyway.

"A guinea pig?" said Mom. "You already have a furry pet."

Stink went to try Dad.

"A guinea pig?" said Dad. "What is it with you kids and guinea pigs? And what about Toady?"

"Have you ever tried to cuddle a toad?" Stink asked.

But it was no use. Astro had just become Astro-NOT.

STINK'S FURRY FACTS

PIG VAN WINKLE

MOST GUINEA PIGS LIVE FOUR TO EIGHT YEARS. THE OLDEST GUINEA PIG ON RECORD IS **SNOWBALL**.

HOME OF THE WORLD'S OLDEST GUINEA PIG

NOTTINGHAMSHIRE, ENGLAND

LIVED TO BE A WHOPPING **14** YEARS AND **10** MONTHS OLD!

14? THAT'S A GUINEA PIG TEENAGER!

WE'LL MISS YOU, SNOWBALL

FEB 1979

Knock, Knock— Who's There?

Stink and his friends knocked on doors all over Webster's neighborhood. "How would you like to adopt a guinea pig?" Stink asked at one house, holding up a box full of wiggly piggies.

"No, thanks. We already have three dogs."

They knocked on another door. "They're really cute," said Sophie, holding one up.

"They're really, *really* cute!" said Webster.

"My son has allergies. Animals with fur make him sneeze."

They knocked on another door. "Come back when you're selling Girl Scout cookies!"

And yet another. "What *is* it?" one lady asked.

"A guinea pig," said Stink.

"I can't have pigs in the house," the lady said.

"Not an *oink-oink* pig," said Stink.

"A furry pet," said Webster. "Like a hamster."

"Actually, guinea pigs are rodents," said Stink, holding one up. The guinea pig wiggled his way right out of Stink's grasp and dropped onto the floor of the lady's house.

"A rodent! Get that rat out of my house!" The lady chased the speedy guinea pig around her living room

with a broom. Finally, she swept it out
the door and Stink scooped it up.

"Phew, that was a close one," he
said to the guinea pig.

* * *

At the next house, Stink said, "Hi, I'm Stink Moody, and—"

"Did you say your name is Moody?" asked the old guy at the door. "Didn't I read about you in the paper? Aren't you the one with the cat that makes toast?"

"That's my sister," said Stink.

"Do these little critters make toast, too? I'd like to see that."

"I don't think so," said Stink.

"No toast, eh? Thanks anyway," the man said, shaking his head.

"Let's try that apartment building," said Webster. They rang a bell on the first floor.

"Guinea pigs, huh? You got any more? I'll take fifty," said the guy at the door. He wasn't wearing a shirt and had a blue tattoo of a cobra on his arm.

"Really? You will? That's great! Are you sure?" said Stink.

"Sure, I'm sure," said the man, grinning under his hairy mustache.

Just then, Sophie nudged her friends and pointed to a van in the parking lot. Across the top it said SQUAMATA

Serpentes. Sam the Snake Man. Snakes of all sizes for your classroom or party.

"Hey, wait a minute," said Webster. "You're that guy who came to school to talk about—"

"Snakes!" said Stink. "And their habits, like what they eat. Um, sorry, mister, we gotta go."

"Yeah, I think maybe my house is on fire!" said Webster, sniffing the air.

"Good save," said Sophie as they hurried away from the building.

"That guy gave me the creeps," said Webster.

"He gave me the squirmy-wormies,"

said Sophie. "His van should say *Squirm*-ata Serpentes." Stink and Webster cracked up.

The three friends sat down on the curb. "We knocked on fifty million doors and didn't find a good home for one single fur ball," said Sophie.

"Think," said Stink. "Where would we find a lot of people in one place?"

"Church!" said Webster.

"Guinea pigs can't go to church," said Stink. "I mean a place people go if they love animals."

Webster snapped his fingers. "I got it! The pet cemetery!"

"Live animals, Webster. We want to make people happy, not sad."

"How about the dog park? People there love animals."

"Yeah, and *dogs* love *guinea pigs*. Pretty soon all the guinea pigs *would* be in the pet cemetery."

Stink thought and thought. Finally, he said, "Time for Operation Guinea Pig!"

"Uh-oh," said Sophie.

"Uh-oh," said Webster.

Squeals on Wheels

On Saturday morning, Judy asked, "Stink, where are you going?"

"For your information, I have a job."

"A job? Snore pie with yawn sauce!" said Judy.

"For your information, my job is way NOT-boring."

"Is it smelly? You got a job smelling with that nose of yours?"

"For your information, it *is* a little smelly. It's at Fur & Fangs, in the G.P. department."

"The Giant Pest department?" Judy asked.

"For your information, it's in the Guinea Pig Department."

"Why are you so . . . green?"

"For your information, I'm wearing all green because it's a guinea pig's favorite color."

"For my information, how much money do you make?"

"None," said Stink.

"Wait. You mean my little brother, Stink 'Make-Money' Moody, took a smelly job at the *pest* store for no money? What for?"

"For *fun,*" said Stink. "Mrs. B. has an old camper behind Fur & Fangs. Webster, Sophie, and I are going to fix it up and turn it into a guinea pig hotel on wheels."

"Like the bookmobile at the library?" Judy asked.

"Yeah, only it'll be the Piggymobile. We'll park it in front of the shopping center where there are tons of people and try to get them to adopt guinea pigs. Except for maybe Astro."

"Rare!" said Judy. "A mini guinea pig zoo."

"The Guinea Pig Express!" said Stink.

✳ ✳ ✳

Stink met Sophie and Webster at Fur & Fangs.

"I brought bungee cords," said Webster.

"I brought goose tape," said Sophie.

"I brought buckets, sponges, and a three-week supply of jawbreakers," said Stink. "In case we get hungry."

Out back, they unloaded every last guinea pig cage. Then they soaped and scrubbed the camper, inside and out, top to bottom. "Car wash!" yelled Webster, squirting Sophie with the hose.

"Not my glasses!" said Sophie.

"You need windshield wipers!" said Stink.

Inside the camper, Sophie stuffed the cupboards with supplies. Webster filled bins with pine shavings and grass hay. Stink poured pellets into trash cans.

They lined each cage with pine shavings, then added food dishes and water bottles with sippy tubes. Stink collected rocks for climbing over, while Sophie and Webster made fun hiding places.

Mrs. B. helped stack cages along one wall inside the camper. There were cages on the counter and one in the sink. There were two under the table and three in the loft. There was even a stack in the shower.

When all the cages were stacked and bungee-corded into place, the kids plopped down in the booth, tired and hungry. Stink pulled out a fistful of jawbreakers.

"I can't believe we fit thirty-three cages in here," said Stink.

"It's a traveling guinea pig palace," said Sophie.

"A piggy parade," said Webster.

"Squeals on Wheels!" yelled Stink.

* * *

The following Saturday, the three friends painted the camper. Sophie painted suns and rainbows and guinea pigs riding unicorns. Webster painted moons and planets and guinea pigs riding rocket ships.

Stink painted eyes—giant blue guinea pig eyes like Astro's—just above the headlights on the front of the RV. And a pink nose and whiskers and a sticky-out tuft of hair above the nose.

"Awesome!" said Webster.

"Fur-eeky!" said Sophie.

The kids wrote SQUEALS ON WHEELS in big letters across the side of the camper. On the back was a bumper sticker that read: VIRGINIA IS FOR LOVERS. Stink changed it to read VIRGINIA IS FOR GUINEA PIG LOVERS.

"Done," said Sophie.

"Wow," said Webster.

"*Purr*-fect," said Mrs. Birdwistle.

Jelly Bean, Pumpkin, Piggy Wiggy, Captain Jack, Hopscotch, Izzy, Fuzzy, Wuzzy, Rapunzel, Skunk, Curly Sue, Wrinkles, Ruby, John, Paul, George,

Ringo, Midnight, Mimi, Mr. Nibbles, Blackberry, Scamper, Scarlett O'Hairy, Harry, Butterscotch, Shredded Wheat, Snowball, Hash Brown, Violet, Miss Piggy . . . They named all 101 guinea pigs and loaded them into cages, sixteen cages for the boys and seventeen cages for the girls. Each cage had a list of who was inside to help keep them all straight.

Soon 101 guinea pigs sipped at their water bottles, rattled their cage doors, and chased each other, playing hide-and-seek to their little hearts' content.

The GuineaPig Whisperer

Beep, *beep! Beep, beep, beep!* Mrs. B. drove like crazy around the parking lot, honking the horn to get people's attention. Then she parked under a big shade tree right next to a busy coffee shop.

"Say hello to Squeals on Wheels!" called Mrs. Birdwistle.

"Ladies and Gentlemen, the Great Guinea Pig Giveaway! Adopt a guinea pig," Stink called. "Or two. Or Three. How about four fur balls?"

"I hope all one hundred and one guinea pigs get adopted soon," said Webster.

"Except for you, Astro," said Stink, whispering to his favorite guinea pig.

Kids and parents crowded into the camper. "Who wants to pet a guinea pig?" asked Stink.

"Me! Me! Me!" yelled all the kids.

"Okay, Guinea Pigs 101: Never grab a guinea pig by the fur on its neck," said Stink, "or you'll scare it. Hold a piggy from underneath, like this."

"Brush your guinea pig every day," said Sophie.

"And feed them fresh fruits and veggies," said Webster, "you know, like parsley and cherry tomatoes."

"Tug of war!" said Stink as Snickers and Oreo raced to munch a bunch of parsley Webster tossed into their cage.

Two girls wearing ponytails and matching headbands asked, "Do you have any twin guinea pigs? We like everything twins."

"We have Fuzzy and Wuzzy!" Sophie showed them two brown-and-white pups with curly ears. Fuzzy and Wuzzy wiggled their fluffy white butts.

"They look like they're wearing tutus," said one twin.

"We'll take them!" said the other.

"Only ninety-nine more to go!" said Sophie.

A tall lady with black-and-white hair and red shoes chose a white-crested guinea pig.

"That lady looked just like Cruella De Vil," said Stink.

"And the guinea pig she picked looked just like *her*," said Webster.

"At least she wasn't wearing a fur coat," said Sophie.

"Take home a guinea pig," yelled Stink. "Take two. Take three. Guinea pigs are happier with a friend!"

"We'll take five," said Parker, a kid Stink knew from Virginia Dare School. He was with his little brother, Cody.

"Score!" said Stink, scooping up the guinea pigs they picked out. They chose Butterscotch, Blackberry, Hash Brown, Jelly Bean, and . . . Astro!

"Sorry. You can't have that one," said Stink.

"Why not?" asked Parker.

"You just can't," Stink said.

"Is he yours?"

"Not *exactly*," said Stink.

"Well, whose is he?"

"Nobody's, but—look, there are ninety-nine million guinea pigs here. Midnight has a black patch over one eye like a pirate. Shredded Wheat has tons of hair. And Snowball's super-friendly." Cody started to cry. He wanted Astro and only Astro.

No way did Stink want to give up Astro. But he knew the time would come when he'd have to, and he didn't want to blow his chance to give away FIVE guinea pigs. Stink took a deep breath. "You'll be okay, boy," he whispered into Astro's ear. "I'll come visit you, I promise." Stink handed him over.

All afternoon, people streamed into Squeals on Wheels, asking questions and peering into cages to watch guinea pigs run and hide and eat and play and nap. By the end of the day, the Guinea Pig Express had found homes for seventeen guinea pigs!

Stink felt sad about Astro. But he was proud they'd found so many good families to take care of guinea pigs.

"Good job!" said Mrs. Birdwistle.

"Knock, knock! Is the Guinea Pig Express still open? I brought you *two* more customers," said Judy. "Rocky and Frank."

"We both want to adopt a guinea pig," said Rocky. Stink passed guinea pigs to Judy's friends.

"Hey! This one doesn't have a tail," said Rocky.

"Guinea pigs don't have tails," said Stink.

"Mine looks like Chewbacca from *Star Wars*!" said Frank Pearl.

"He's called a silkie," said Stink. "Because he's way hairy."

"He looks like a rug," said Judy.

"Hey, Chewy!" said Frank, stroking the little guy.

Wee, wee, wee, wee, wee! "My guy sure is noisy," said Rocky.

"That just means it's hungry," said Stink.

"Stink, since when do you speak guinea pig?" Judy asked. "Ooh, it's like you're the Guinea Pig Whisperer or something."

"Or something," said Stink. "If your

guinea pig goes *Arr! Arr!* and barks like a seal, that means it's lonely. And purring means—"

"Your guinea pig got eaten by a cat?" Judy asked.

"No! It means it's curious. If it goes *Pttp! Pttp!* like a tiny trumpet, that means it's happy. *Rrrrrrrrr!*" Stink trilled, like a car motor.

"What's that one mean?"

"That your guinea pig's in the best mood ever," said Stink. "It means, *Ooh-la-la!*"

And Then There Were Five

Nineteen guinea pigs! Stink was feeling pleased as punch all weekend about the Great Guinea Pig Giveaway.

Until Monday at school, that is. Parker stopped Stink in the hall. "We have to give back our guinea pigs," Parker said. "Both Hash Brown and Butterscotch chewed holes in the new sofa. Blackberry made a nest out of my sister's doll's hair. And Jelly Bean ate a whole bag of jelly beans and made rainbow poop in my mom's go-to-work shoes."

Stink couldn't help laughing. "What about Astro?"

"Astro tiptoed across my dad's computer keyboard and e-mailed his boss by mistake."

"Good boy!" said Stink. "I mean, too bad. Well, you'll just have to take them back to Mrs. Birdwistle."

"Can't you take them? My mom'll freak if I bring them home again."

"My mom will freak, too," said Stink. He peered at the squirming heap of fur balls. Astro looked up at him and made a tiny trumpet sound. Stink's heart melted.

"Never mind. I'll take them back for you."

Parker handed over the cardboard carrier to Stink.

"Astro!" Stink whispered to his furry friend. "You came back!"

* * *

The five guinea pigs slept their way through social studies, ran their way through recess, and squeaked up a storm all the way through Mrs. D.'s exciting reading of *The Mouse and the Motorcycle*.

On the way home, Stink told Judy what happened. "Do you think if I ask super-duper nice this time, Mom and Dad might let me keep Astro?"

"Yes," said Judy. "When guinea pigs *fly*."

"Hardee-har-har," said Stink. "But I'm serious. I let Astro go and he came back. It's a sign."

"A sign that you're cuckoo if you think you can keep him."

When Stink got home, he rushed up to his room before his mother could see him and slid the carrier under his bed. Maybe he could hide them for just a little while. How hard could it be to hide a few furry critters?

He ran down to the kitchen and piled salad greens and a baby carrot, a strawberry, and a melon cube on a plate. "Good for you, Stink," said Mom. "A healthy snack for once, instead of all those jawbreakers."

"Uh-huh," said Stink. He hurried back upstairs to his room.

Judy met him in the hall. "Stink, I wouldn't go in there if I were you," she said, blocking the doorway.

Stink tried to see past her. "What do you mean?"

"Your underwear, Stink. It's *alive!*"

Stink pushed past her, and Judy followed. A pair of underpants dashed across the floor, up and over his bed, and around the legs of his desk.

"Holy underwear!" Judy yelled. She jumped out of the way.

"Attack of the Mutant Undies!" said Stink, chasing the runaway underpants around his room. "Helppp!"

Judy helped Stink corner the undies behind his wastebasket. Stink pounced on the undies. "Gotcha!" Up popped Astro's head through a leg hole.

"Look over there!" Judy said. Four more guinea pigs were peeking up out of Stink's bottom dresser drawer. "It's the Brotherhood of the Traveling Undies."

"You guys are going to get me busted," said Stink, putting them all back into the carrier. "Stay in there, Astro, you hear me?"

"I'm outta here," said Judy in a squeaky-high voice, pretending to be Astro. "This place is really stinky."

"Very funny, Judy," said Stink.

"Stink, you're the one who's a Guinea Pig Whisperer. You can hear guinea pigs talk, remember? That wasn't me. That was Astro."

"Oh, yeah? What's he saying right now?"

Judy held her ear up to the carrier. "He's saying, 'Help! Save me! I have a piggly-wiggly wedgie!'"

STINK'S FURRY FACTS

GUINEA PIG HALL OF FAME

DID YOU KNOW?

QUEEN ELIZABETH I HAD A PET GUINEA PIG!

TEDDY ROOSEVELT HAD **5** GUINEA PIGS AT THE WHITE HOUSE! THEY WERE ALL NAMED AFTER REAL PEOPLE!

ONE OF HIS KIDS ONCE INTERRUPTED A MEETING BY SHOUTING...

FATHER! COME QUICKLY! BISHOP DOANE JUST HAD BABIES!!

Virginia
Beach
or Bust!

After the Attack of the Mutant Undies, Stink took all five guinea pigs back to Fur & Fangs and broke the news to Mrs. Birdwistle.

"One hundred and one guinea pigs minus nineteen that were adopted plus five that were brought back equals eighty-seven guinea pigs," Stink said. "You have a lot more fur than fangs."

Mrs. Birdwistle laughed. "There is some good news, though. I have a friend in Virginia Beach who started a guinea pig rescue. She says she can take about twenty guinea pigs if I can get them to her."

"Virginia Beach!" said Stink. "I'll go!"

"Aren't you a little too short to drive?" Mrs. B. asked.

"But *you* could drive!" said Stink. "Webster and Sophie and I can find homes for guinea pigs along the way!"

"Wait just a minute," said Mrs. B. "You're saying you want me to drive you and a rattletrap camper full of one hundred and one guinea pigs all the way to Virginia Beach?"

"Eighty-seven guinea pigs," said Stink.

"It's a great idea!" said Mrs. B.

VIRGINIA BEACH OR BUST!

* * *

On the day of the trip, Mrs. B. handed the kids a map. "Let's each choose one place to stop where we might be able to find homes for guinea pigs."

Mrs. B. pointed to Bull Run Castle.

Webster chose the Reston Zoo. Sophie picked the mermaid fountains in Norfolk. And Stink chose Smithfield, home of the World's Biggest Ham.

"Let's get this show on the road," said Mrs. B., and they all piled into the camper. But Violet didn't want to stay in her cage. Midnight hid under the seat. And Miss Piggy ate half a bag of chips before they even started.

It was going to be one wild ride. The kids sang at the top of their lungs.

"Eighty-seven guinea pigs rolling along,
Eighty-seven guinea pigs.
Take some down, pass 'em around,

Eighty-seven guinea pigs rolling along . . ."

* * *

First stop was Bull Run Castle.

"It was built to be somebody's house once," said Mrs. B. "But now it's a museum. And people can rent it out for parties and events."

"Look!" said Stink. "A bunch of kids dressed up like witches and wizards."

Six kids from a Harry Potter party talked their parents into letting them have guinea pigs!

* * *

Next stop, the Reston Zoo.

At the elephant house, Stink saw the most amazing animal that wasn't even an elephant. It was the world's biggest guinea pig!

"The sign says it's a capybara," said Mrs. B. "It comes from South America,

just like guinea pigs do, and it's the world's largest living rodent. Scientists found a skeleton of one rodent relative that's eight million years old. The 'giant rat' weighed fifteen hundred pounds."

"*Guinea giganticus!*" said Stink, making up a scientific name.

When they got back to Squeals on Wheels, people were peering through the windows of the camper at all the guinea pigs.

"Get your cute guinea pigs here," they announced. In no time, Squeals on Wheels was a little less squeal-y.

* * *

Stink studied the map. "Next stop—world's biggest ham!"

After crossing over the James River Bridge, they pulled into Smithfield, Virginia—Pig City, USA.

"There it is!" said Stink. "The museum with the pet ham."

Inside the museum, displayed in a glass case, was a small, wrinkly lump covered in green mold.

"Gross!" said Sophie. "It looks like a shrunken head."

"Double gross!" said Webster. "It looks like a giant turd. Maybe we came to the World's Biggest Turd Museum by mistake."

"I don't get it," said Stink. "The sign says it's more than one hundred years old. See? Oh, I get it now. It's the world's *oldest* ham, not biggest."

"Does the sign say it's super-disgusting?" said Webster.

A half hour later, they left the ham museum.

"We didn't even adopt out one single guinea pig," said Sophie.

"Yeah, 'cause in this town they all like *ham*-sters," Stink said.

* * *

Over bridges, across rivers, and through a dark tunnel they drove until Mrs. B. pulled up to a big fountain in the middle of Norfolk. They let Izzy, Scarlett O'Hairy, Harry, Captain Jack, Hopscotch, Piggy

Wiggy, Wrinkles, Pumpkin, Mimi, and Mr. Nibbles wade in the fountain. Astro, too.

"Super-suds city!" screeched Webster. "Somebody must have put soap in the fountain."

"Hey, let's give the guinea pigs a bubble bath!" said Sophie.

Webster and Stink and Sophie washed and dried and fluffed the eleven guinea pigs.

"Get your squeaky-clean guinea pigs here," they yelled, and ten more of the world's cleanest guinea pigs left for new homes.

"Fifty-nine guinea pigs rolling along . . ."

STINK'S FURRY FACTS

FAT RAT?

WHAT ROLLS IN THE MUD AND LOOKS LIKE A HIPPO...

MUD BATH

IS AS BIG AS STINK...

HAS WEBBED FEET, LIKES TO EAT BARK...

No, NOT MY SISTER!

KNOWS HOW TO WHISTLE, AND CAN SLEEP UNDERWATER?

IS IT A DUCK? A PIG?

A HIPPO?

NOPE! IT'S THE WORLD'S LARGEST RODENT AND COUSIN TO THE GUINEA PIG...

HI, CUZ!

THE CAPYBARA!

This Little Piggy

Another seventeen miles down the road, at last they hit Virginia Beach! A big green sign said:

MT. TRASHMORE

"What's Mt. Trashmore? Is it really a mountain?" asked Webster.

"Is it a park?" asked Sophie.

"Is it really made of trash?" Stink slid open the window and sniffed.

"Mt. Trashmore used to be a huge garbage dump," said Mrs. B. "But then they covered it up with layers of soil, turning it into a kind of big hill or mountain. And now it's a park."

"Whoa," said Stink. "A giant trash sandwich."

At Mt. Trashmore, kids and families were fishing, feeding ducks, flying kites, skateboarding, and racing remote-controlled boats off the pier.

They found homes for fourteen guinea pigs at Mt. Trashmore alone.

* * *

Virginia Beach was pig heaven. *Guinea pig* heaven, that is. People went gaga for guinea pigs in this town.

At the Beatles Museum, they gave away John, Paul, George, and Ringo. At Ocean Breeze Water Park, they gave away zero. But they got to see a giant gorilla named Hugh Mongous. At the amusement park they gave away eight more. Plus, one lady

adopted ten because she kept falling in love with one, and then another, and then another.

"Virginia Beach rocks," Webster said.

"Operation Guinea Pig rocks!" said Stink.

"Time to get back to Squeals on Wheels," said Mrs. Birdwistle. "Next stop, my friend Daisy's house."

But when they got to the camper, something was not right. The horn was honking. The radio was blasting. The windshield wipers were wiping.

Great balls of fur! Twenty-three guinea pigs were on the loose. Those hair balls were having one big piggy party. "Hurry, Mrs. B.! Guinea pigs are going bonkers in there!"

"Holey tamoley!" screeched Webster when he saw Mrs. B.'s coffee thermos knocked over. "The guinea pigs drank your coffee!"

Hyperdrive! The Guinea Pig Express had turned into the Guinea Pig Espresso. Guinea pigs were here, there, and everywhere, poking out of every box, bag, backpack, cupboard, and cubbyhole.

Guinea pigs ran races around the camper. Guinea pigs spun circles on the counters. Guinea pigs slipped and slid into the empty sink. Curly Sue went snooping in the closet!

All three kids chased after the

squirming fur balls and put them back in their cages.

After they finished cleaning up the mess, Mrs. B. said, "Phew! Last stop— my friend Daisy's house!"

On the way to the rescue, Astro poked his head out of Stink's backpack. "This is it, boy," said Stink, rubbing noses with his favorite fur ball. "I'm going to miss you, boy."

Mrs. Birdwistle's friend, Daisy, met them at the front door. "Aren't they adorable?" she cooed.

"We have twenty-three left," said Stink. "How many can you take?"

"Twenty-three's fine."

"Are you sure? Twenty-*two* is a much better number. Twenty-three just sounds like one too many."

"I'm sure," said Daisy. "Three more won't be a problem at all."

"I'm afraid these little guys are escape artists," Mrs. B. told her.

"And they're hyper on coffee!" said Webster.

"I have just the thing to wear them out," Daisy said, and pointed to a play area on the floor.

"A mini amusement park!" said Sophie. There was a guinea pig Ferris

wheel, a super slide, even a haunted house. Soon guinea pigs were tearing through tunnels, racing over rocks, hiding in hideouts.

"See? They're getting tired out already," said Daisy.

Stink said good-bye to Astro. "You'll be fine, boy," he whispered around the lump in his throat. "Virginia Beach is a great place to live."

"Oops, I almost forgot," said Daisy. "I have something for you." She handed them T-shirts that said "Guinea Pig Power."

Webster, Sophie, and Stink thanked Daisy. Mrs. B. hugged her friend good-bye and thanked her, too.

"Time to go!" said Mrs. B. "We have a long drive home." The kids scooped up their backpacks and climbed into the camper.

Stink stared at the empty cages. What fun was a Piggymobile without any piggies? Or Squeals on Wheels without any squeals? A camper without cavies was like an encyclo-pedia without the letter *S*.

STINK'S FURRY FACTS: TOLEDO OR BUST!

GREAT MINDS THINK ALIKE! GUINEA PIG RESCUERS FROM CALIFORNIA LOADED MORE THAN ONE HUNDRED FUR BALLS INTO A WINNEBAGO NICKNAMED **THE PIGGYBAGO!**

From California to Ohio!

PiggyBago
Toledo • Bust!

THE TRIP LASTED **11** DAYS.

CALIFORNIA

OHIO

THEY FOUND HOMES FOR THE GUINEA PIGS ALONG THE WAY!

5,700 MILES ROUND TRIP!
WOW!

All the Way Home

When Stink got home, he gave his family a souvenir—a box of saltwater taffy. And he told Mom, Dad, and Judy every last little thing about his trip, everything from the Town of Ham to the giant bubble-bath fountain to Mt. Trashmore to the guinea pig amusement park.

Mom could not stop laughing over the coffee caper in the camper. Judy tried to laugh, but her teeth were stuck together from all the saltwater taffy.

"I wish I got Judy taffy a long time ago!" Stink joked. "That's the longest I ever got to talk in my whole life without her butting in."

As long as Stink's family was laughing and telling stories, Stink missed Astro and the other guinea pigs a little bit less.

Mouse came into the kitchen, dragging Stink's backpack along, a strap held between her teeth.

"Hey, Mouser!" said Stink. "Yes, that's my backpack. Yes, I'm home now."

"I can't believe it," said Judy. "I can't believe she actually came out from under my bed. She's been moping there the whole time you were gone, like she was in a bad mood or something."

"Did you miss me, girl?" asked Stink, tugging on his backpack. But Mouse would not give it up.

"Weird," said Judy.

"Strange," said Mom.

"I need my backpack, Mouse," said Stink. "You're going to have to give it back sooner or later."

"Yeah, sooner," said Judy. "Because we have school tomorrow and I bet you didn't do your homework yet!"

"Stink, is that true?" asked Dad.

"Well . . . see . . ." said Stink.

Just then, Mouse made a funny sound. Everybody got quiet. The funny sound sounded like a purr, but the purr wasn't coming from Mouse. No, the funny sound was coming from Stink's backpack.

There was only one thing Stink knew that purred like a cat but wasn't a cat. He reached into his backpack and scooped out a tiny ball of fur, the cutest hair ball he'd ever seen.

"Astro!" said Stink, nuzzling noses with his favorite fur ball. "I don't get it—you're supposed to be in Virginia Beach." Stink sat on the floor, held Astro in his lap, and scratched him under the chin.

"Stink! You kept him and brought him back?" Judy asked.

"Stink, I thought we agreed—" Dad started.

"I didn't keep him! Honest! I didn't even know he was in there. He must have stowed away in my backpack for the whole ride home."

"One cat plus one guinea pig equals *Trouble* with a capital *T*," said Judy.

Just then, Mouse crawled onto Stink's lap. "Mouse, no!" shouted Stink. But Mouse only licked Astro from top to bottom, just as if the guinea pig were a tiny kitten.

Dad looked at Mom. Mom looked at Dad. And before Stink could even ask, they both nodded. As in *Y-E-S*, he could keep Astro!

Ooh-la-la. Stink was in pig heaven. Guinea pig heaven, that is.

Astro-nomical!

Adopting a guinea pig—or any pet—is a big decision. Make sure you understand the time, care, and cost involved before making a final commitment and bringing any critters home! If you are interested in learning more about owning and caring for guinea pigs, ask your local librarian to recommend an authoritative and reputable guide. To learn more about guinea pig rescue in your area, visit www.guinealynx.info and click on "Rescues."